Mandy Sue Day

With love to my husband,
my sons Armin and Jason,
and my parents.
—*R.K.*

Clarion Books
a Houghton Mifflin Company imprint
215 Park Avenue South, New York, NY 10003
Text copyright © 1994 by Roberta Karim
Illustrations copyright © 1994 by Karen Ritz

The illustrations for this book were executed in watercolor
on Fabriano hot-press watercolor paper.
The text was set in 14-point Palatino.

Printed in the USA

Library of Congress Cataloging-in-Publication Data

Karim, Roberta.
Mandy Sue Day / by Roberta Karim ; illustrated by Karen Ritz.
p.   cm.
Summary: Using her senses of taste, hearing, touch, and smell, a blind girl enjoys a special day on the farm.
ISBN 0-395-66155-2   PA ISBN 0-618-31675-2
[1. Blind—Fiction. 2. Physically handicapped—Fiction. 3. Farm life—Fiction.] I. Ritz, Karen, ill.   II. Title.
PZ7.K1384Man 1994
[E]—dc20   93-34671
CIP
AC

BVG   10 9 8 7 6 5 4

Mandy Sue Day

By Roberta Karim
Illustrated by Karen Ritz

Clarion Books / *New York*

Morning wind tickles my ear.
My eyes blink open.
Down in the cornfield, crows caw
        and caw.
I sing along:
        Today's the day
        Yahoo Hooray
        Mandy Sue Day
            today!

Harvesting's hard work here
        on Amos Acres.
A mama and a papa and
five brothers and sisters
all bringing in the bounty.
Combines and calluses.
Pressing cider and
putting up pumpkins.

But I remember Papa's promise:
"A week's worth of Indian summer
is dropping by!" he said.
"One day off to each of you children
for good behavior."
And today is MY day!

Bacon for breakfast
and no schoolin' after lunch.
Yahoo Hooray for Mandy Sue Day!

"Will Ben take good care of you?"
asks Papa.
"Best friends always do,"
says Mama. "*Shoo!*"

I'm out the screen door. *Slam.*
Squeak goes the third step.
I canter to the barn,
fingers ticking off the fence posts.
Twenty-four to the old barn door.

Ben whinnies low. I whinny back.
Nineteen steps, or eight bunny hops,
to Ben's Dutch door.
Today I hop.
Impatient, Ben snuffs my hand.
He noses up my arm, my neck,
blows windily in my ear.
"No carrot there, Ben.
You lose.
Today it's hiding in my boot."

Ben grumbles with delight.
I squeeze the fat carrot top.
Strong teeth tug the bottom.
Closer and closer
comes the chomping.
At the last second, I make a palm.
Ben gulps down the carrot top.
For dessert,
he polishes my hand
with his tongue.
"What do I look like?" I ask him.
"A salt block?"

Halter click-clacking.
Ben's deep in his bucket.
Slurp of water. Slurp of air.
"Time for a refill, Ben?"

My fingers brush along rough wood,
out to the smooth pump handle.
Water gurgles up from the earth,
whooshes down to the bucket.
Metal handle digs deep in my hand.

On Tuesday, Mama taught us
centrifugal force.
Will it hold true on Wednesday?
I start to spin.

Soon the pail is flying sideways,
but not a drop of water spills.
Must be mashed to the sides,
like Little Jeremy and me
on the fair's Whirly-Gig.

Ben snorts a "where-have-you-been?"
"Here's your water, Carrot Breath."
Noisy gulps slow to splashes
and I know he's playing in his water.
"Sillier than Baby May
in the kitchen sink,"
I tell him.

"Grooming time, Ben. Curry first."
Round rows of metal teeth
circle and circle his coat,
        stirring up loose hairs,
        rubbing his tummy.
"You're one big dust cloud," I scold.
His withers twitch.

"Stiff brush, Ben.
Hold on to your skin."
Two hands for one brush,
and the hairs and dust fly.
AH-CHOO.

Soft brush last, silky coat.

Now the knotted mane.
I sigh like Mama.
"Been chewing gum
in your sleep again, Benjamin?"

Triple-knotted tail.
"You've tangled with every fly
in the county, Ben Boy."

Hoof pick's in my hand,
so Ben plants his foot.
I shove him off balance,
clean stones from the Vs.

Smooth out the wrinkles on the
Navajo blanket.
Fly the heavy saddle up and over,
stirrups swinging like a runaway.

Ben puffs up his belly,
all stubborn against the cinch,
but he's no match
for a bony kneecap.
I serve up his bridle
with a cube of sugar.
He falls for it, as usual.

Ben jangles his hardware
and paws the dirt.
"Hold your horses, Crazy One.
Let me get on."
At the stone wall
      I feel for footing,
      feel for a stirrup,
      fling myself up.

Out in the lane,
hooves clip-clopping,
crunching leaves.
I jump
as something brushes my cheek.
What was that?
        I reach out—
        it's raining leaves!

Slide into cool.
We're in the woods.
I hug Ben's neck.
No twigs stinging *my* face, no sirree.
I pat his shoulder,
hard muscles working
under soft skin.
He jumps.
"Rabbit cross your path, Ben?"

Burst into warm.
We're out of the woods.
Ben stops.
I stand in my stirrups
to touch his ears.
They're pricked forward,
listening to the meadow beyond.
"I love you, Ben."
His ears flick back to catch my voice.

One nudge and
we're off in a bouncy trot.
He gathers steam,
breaks into a rocking-horse canter
that takes my breath away.
I bend low.
My knees grip hard.
He hits a gallop, and I'm a Sioux,
racing across the plains.
We're one with the wind.
I'm one with him
or I'd fall to the herd
of trampling buffalo.

Whiffs of wood smoke
and Concord grapes.
We're almost home.
Ben slows to a walk.
Clatter clatter up the stone path.
"I smell donuts!"
Ben's already busy
untying my half hitch.
He *does* love a kettle-fried donut.
Mama brings out cider for me.
Melted apples slidin' down slow.
"Need any help, Mama?"
"No child, you frolic.
This is Mandy Sue Day all day,
remember?"

I land on Ben.
"Drive me to the barn, taxi."
He pulls up at the trough
to wash down his donut.

Off with the bridle.
Off with the saddle
and Navajo blanket.
Pick off the burrs.
"Post time, Ben."
Barn door bangs open and he's off,
pounding the path.
I straddle the top rail and wait.
Soon he's back to nuzzle my knee.
I slide on.
He wanders and I weave my fingers
through his mane.
He bends to graze
and I lie back on his rump.
The wind blows full of wild roses
and warm horse.

BONG BONG BONG.
The dinner bell calls
all hands from the fields.
One scoop of oats,
one scoop of sweet feed,
half bale of hay.
Evening water weighs way too much
to measure centrifugal force.
"Gate's open," calls my brother.

"You've outdone yourself, Ma,"
say my brothers.
Food swirls by.
Fried chicken, mashed potatoes,
biscuits and gravy,
tomato-and-cuke salad,
sweet corn by the bushel.
"And for dessert?" they hint.
"Peach pie with a candle," she says.
They sing in three keys:
"Happy Mandy Sue Day to you."
"Mama and Papa," I say,
"since it's still my day,
could I sleep in the loft tonight?"

"Well." I hear their smiles meet.
"Ben will take care of her,"
says Papa.
"That's what best friends are for,"
says Mama.

Soon she says, her voice muffled,
"Here's your pillow, sheets, and quilt.
Let's carry these out to the basket, Pa."
His chair scrapes back.

Mama, Papa, and I
step through the crisp evening.
The screen door bangs.
Papa turns.
"Whatcha got there, Little Jeremy?"
"Flashlight for Mandy Sue."
"Oh." Papa's voice smiles.
I answer, "I don't need one, Little J.
Remember?
I can't see."

"Oh." Jeremy's voice thinks.
"Well, how about a peppermint stick?"
"Thanks, Jeremy."
"Sweet dreams, Mandy Sue."

Papa's arm around me,
no need to count fence posts.

Hand over hand,
I climb the loft ladder.
Hand over hand,
I draw up the basket of bedding.

Soon, snug in the straw,
my hand burrows
down to the floorboard crack.
"I love you, Ben," I call down.
"Sweet dreams."

And in the darkness,
I can see his ears flick
to catch my voice.